# Oddies

This book belongs to:

..................................................

Oddies Limited, Maritime House, Grafton Square, London, SW4 0JP
www.oddieworld.com

A CIP catalogue record for this book is available from the British Library.

First Published in Great Britain in 2004 by Oddies Limited.

ISBN 1-904745-11-3

Printed in China

# The Story of
# Oddieworld

Grant Slatter

Once upon a time there was a wizard who had two daughters.

One was a naughty witch.

The other was a good fairy.

They all lived together in a house in the woods, but not very happily. Witch and Fairy were always squabbling. It gave the wizard a headache!

One day the wizard looked in his spell book and saw a spell called the Oddie Spell. It could make people the best of friends.

The wizard needed five portions of fruit and vegetables. He also needed one of Fairy's socks and one of Witch's socks.

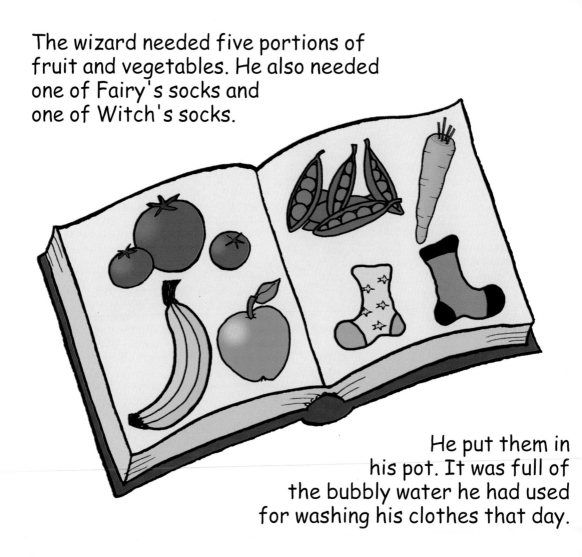

He put them in his pot. It was full of the bubbly water he had used for washing his clothes that day.

Suddenly the wizard noticed one of his own socks in the pot! "Oh there's my missing sock," he said. "I hope my spell will still work."

The socks turned into Oddies.
They called themselves Wizzo, Witchy and Sock Fairy.

They flew off towards a new planet, far away in space.
It was called Oddieworld.

The Oddies came through the Sockhole
and floated down into Oddieworld.
Wizzo looked around him.

"Well, this looks very nice," he said.
"We'll have some fun exploring,
but we must go home before it gets dark."

So they all looked at some of the strange things in Oddieworld.

Wizzo decided it was time to go home.

"*Ipto Birdtome, fly us back home,*" he said.
There was a loud bang and
a big puff of smoke.

When the smoke cleared, Witchy and Sock Fairy giggled. Wizzo's spell had gone wrong and a very big bird was sitting on him.

There was a cosmic bang and a fantastic puff of smoke!

The land split with a big crack. There were now two islands.

Witchy was on one island and Sock Fairy was on the other.

Witchy liked her island and decided to stay. "I'm going to magic lots of bad Oddies here to help me," she said.

Bad Oddie Island

Good Oddie Island

Sock Fairy liked her island and decided to stay. "I'm going to magic lots of good Oddies here to help me," she said.

Back home the wizard went to bed.
He hadn't been able to find a spell which
would bring the three socks back.

He closed his spell book
and asked himself...

"Where did those odd socks go?"

# Have you got the complete collection?

The Story of Oddieworld is just the start of the Oddies' experience. Read the stories of all the other Oddies and their adventures in Oddieworld.

Witchy is cooking up a storm in Oddieworld and Sock Fairy needs some help from **Footy Oddie**, but can he find a way to put things right?

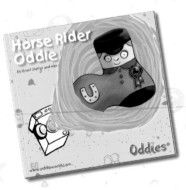

Lucky the horse won't go into her stable so Sock Fairy sends for **Horse Rider Oddie**, but will she spot what is missing from the stable?

Someone has been scribbling on Good Oddie Island so Sock Fairy sends for Police Oddie, but he's having a little trouble finding the culprit.

Witchy wants the Oddie Crown Jewels and calls Robber Oddie to help her get them, but he soon learns that crime doesn't pay.

Litterbug has a tummy ache and nobody knows why, so Sock Fairy sends for Nurse Oddie, but can she make this patient better in a tick?

# Every Oddie has a story to tell!

# Take your child on an adventure...
## ...to Oddieworld!

Visit www.oddieworld.com and help your child gain basic computer skills and have fun at the same time.

- Games
- Puzzles
- Colouring-in
- Free Oddiecards
- Competitions
- Buy Oddies books & 'matching odd socks'

**Please Note:** Use of this website may permanently IMPROVE your child's hand/eye co-ordination and intelligence!

There are lots of
games to play plus
one secret game!

Find it and complete it
and we'll send you a
FREE Oddies poster!

Be quick and you can
win one of the last,
original artwork,
Oddies posters
like this one.

www.**oddieworld**.com

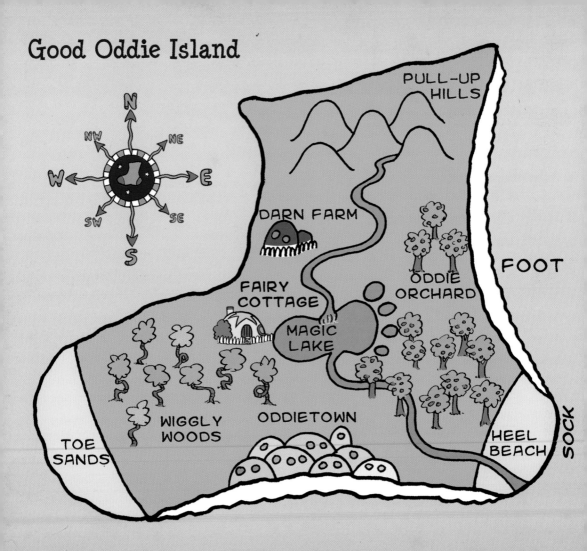